Written by Lynne Suesse, Emily Skwish, and Erin Rose Wage
Illustrated by Animagination, Inc., Art Mawhinney, Lori Tyminski, Adrienne Brown, Studio IBOIX, and the Disney Storybook Art Team

Look and Find®
we make books come alive®

Phoenix International Publications, Inc.
Chicago • London • New York • Hamburg • Mexico City • Paris • Sydney

Sheriff Woody is happy being Andy's favorite toy. Woody and Andy do everything together...until Buzz Lightyear arrives. Buzz is an action figure who thinks he is a real space ranger. After some exciting adventures with mutant toys, aliens, and army soldiers, Woody and Buzz become besties. And, as their story continues, they meet a whole toybox of friends and foes along the way!

Meet the Toys

Woody

The leader of all the toys, Woody is brave and quick-thinking. His competitive streak makes him want to tell Buzz Lightyear, "This town ain't big enough for the two of us," but he has a kind heart. When a toy's in trouble, you've got a friend in Woody.

Buzz Lightyear

Buzz is a high-tech space ranger who is always ready to go to infinity and beyond! When he discovers he is a toy and not a real outer-space hero, he doubts himself for a moment. Then Woody helps him find his true superpower: making Andy happy.

Bo Peep

Bo knows how to stand up for her friends. When the rest of the toys accuse Woody of knocking Buzz out of the window on purpose, she is willing to stand by her Sheriff. She is kind, generous, and especially great with sheep.

Jessie

Jessie is a rootin'-tootin' cowgirl who loves to yodel. She is always ready with a loud "Yee-haw!" when she's happy. She gets nervous in the dark or in small, closed spaces, but when it comes to helping her friends, Jessie never gives up.

Lotso

Lots-o'-Huggin' Bear is cuddly and pink and smells like strawberries, but he has hidden plans to keep Woody, Buzz, and their pals imprisoned in a daycare room full of destructive toddlers. The friends have to find a way to escape from this pink menace.

Forky

The toys' new owner Bonnie makes another friend—out of an old plastic spork and some pipe cleaners. Now Forky is Bonnie's favorite toy. She doesn't know that Woody has to save Forky again and again as he attempts to jump into his happy place, the trash can.

Gabby Gabby

Gabby Gabby is a talking doll who can't talk. Her voice box is broken, and she wants Woody's! She is willing to do whatever it takes to find her voice, including fork-napping Forky. It's up to Woody and the toys to save him. They just might end up helping Gabby Gabby at the same time.

Andy is great at dreaming up new adventures for his toys! Before Andy and Woody leave for Cowboy Camp, Woody must save Bo Peep from the Evil Dr. Porkchop. Buzz Lightyear comes to lend a hand and help Bo Peep escape from a vicious shark and menacing monkeys.

You can help Woody, too. Find Buzz and these other toys that can assist in the daring rescue:

LIGHT

Now it's Woody's turn to need rescuing, but this is no imaginary adventure. A greedy toy collector named Al McWiggen captures Woody from a yard sale and plans to sell him to a museum in Japan. On the way to save Woody, his friends get stuck in some serious traffic. They arrive at the airport in the nick of time!

As Buzz, Hamm, and Rex dodge traffic, look for these fun things that seem a little too familiar:

Buzz Lightyear air freshener

this sign

this dashboard ornament

this cup holder

this license plate

funky monkey fringe

EGGS
MARVO
THE
MARVELOUS
MAGIC
MAGIC
TREES
Joe's Trees
MILK
PIZZA
PIZZA
PIZZA
PIZZA
GROOVY
PEACE
LOVE

Andy is grown up and getting ready to go away to college. He hasn't played with his toys in a long time. When he packs up his boxes, he will bring these things to college instead:

COLLEGE
ATTIC
LEGE

When Andy's toys are donated to Sunnyside Daycare, Lotso assures them that their worries are over. The toys believe it—the Butterfly Room looks like toy heaven! Look around for these other toys that call Sunnyside home:
toy truck
Stretch
Sparks
Big Baby
Chunk
Twitch

7
7
D

The Caterpillar Room isn't as fun as the toys thought it would be! Search for these toys that might be better for the little kids to play with:
xylophone
plastic frying pan
these wooden blocks
big plastic keys
"roller coaster" toy
toy lawn mower
big bouncy ball

Bonnie finds Woody outside of Sunnyside and decides to take him home. She introduces Woody to her other toys and serves them all lunch. Find these colorful items from Bonnie's kitchen set:
purple teapot
blue teacup
pink plate
yellow bowl
red tumbler
green pitcher

Lotso's guards won't let the toys leave the Caterpillar Room. But the guards don't know that Woody has returned to rescue his friends! They don't belong in the storage bins. Find these art supplies that do:
bundle of pipe cleaners
this jar of paint
glue
safety scissors
paintbrush
this box of crayons
jar of glitter

Woody helped his friends escape from the Caterpillar Room. Now they just have to make it across the playground without being spotted by one of the guards. Search the playground to see where they've hidden!

The toys escape Sunnyside in a garbage truck, and the truck dumps them in a landfill. Ending up here is every toy's greatest fear! Hunt for these broken toys that Woody and his friends see:

When Woody realizes that Andy will never forget him, he decides that all the toys should stick together...at Bonnie's house! Look around the yard to find these toys that already live there:

Peatey, Peatrice, and Peanelope

Mr. Pricklepants

Buttercup

Trixie

Chuckles

Dolly

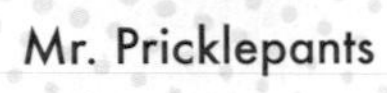

Bonnie's closet doors burst open. The toy town is ready for business! From being the mayor, to running the hat shop, to de-ghosting the haunted bakery, every toy has an important job to do... except Woody. Bonnie doesn't play with him much anymore. He's been left in the closet along with her toddler toys.

HATS
DINOSAUR on the DANCE FLOOR
While Bonnie's imagination runs free, find these hard-working, and hardly working, toys.
Buttercup
Rex
Dolly
Jessie
Hamm
Woody
Trixie
Buzz Lightyear

At kindergarten orientation, Bonnie is nervous. Woody knows Bonnie is worried about starting school, so he stows away in her backpack in case he can help her. During craft time, Woody sees an opportunity when Bonnie is left without art materials.

Help Woody round up these crafty supplies that Bonnie will use to *make* a new friend...named Forky!
spork
red pipe cleaner
rainbow decal
googly eyes
wooden craft stick
this modeling clay
glue
crayons

Forky is Bonnie's favorite toy! He feels most comfortable in the trash, so he hops into every garbage can he finds...and Woody saves him. On a family vacation, the two toys get separated from Bonnie's RV and end up at an antique shop. Woody spots the lamp of his old friend Bo Peep, and he goes searching for her. Instead, he finds Gabby Gabby. Her voice box is broken, and she wants Woody's!

As Woody stares down Gabby Gabby's ventriloquist dummies, shop around for these antiques:

fondue pot
Gabby Gabby
Benson
birdcage
bonnet
this teapot
watering can
trumpet

Woody escapes the antique shop, but Gabby Gabby fork-naps Forky! On a playground outside the shop, Woody encounters a rowdy bunch of Grand Basin Summer Camp kids. Just as he fears for his stitches, he runs into Bo! She's been living as a lost toy with her best pal Officer Giggle McDimples. They agree to help Woody rescue Forky from Gabby Gabby's clutches.

Join in the fun running, stomping, and swinging with these lost, lovable toys:
ice-cream toy
Volcano Attack Combat Carl
Giggle McDimples
Billy, Goat, and Grutt
Combat Carl
dinosaur toy
Ice Attack Combat Carl
Bo Peep
SUMMER CAMP

When Woody and Forky have been gone a long time, the rest of the toys in the RV start to worry. Buzz listens to his inner voice and goes in search of his friends. He crash-lands in a carnival, where a carnival worker mistakes him for a prize. Zip-tied to a wall, Buzz meets some colorful characters named Ducky and Bunny, who don't want Buzz taking their top-toy spot.

X-99
X-99
TICKETS
You must be THIS TALL to Ride!
Before a kid with stellar aim wins them all, look for these premium prizes:
Ducky and Bunny
this ice-cream cone
fox
this rocket
astronaut
Buzz
this yellow star
guitar

Once Buzz finds Woody, the rescue team enters the antique shop together. Down one of the aisles is a pinball machine, which the friends can enter by punching a secret code on the coin return. Inside, tons of toys are unwinding, including Canada's greatest motorcycle daredevil, Duke Caboom! Bo needs him to jump into Gabby Gabby's case, but Duke is nervous. What if he crashes?

Now that Bo has assured Duke that crashing is fine, search through the buzzers and bells for these carefree playthings:

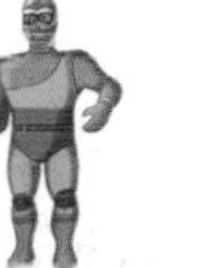

Duke Caboom | Tinny | this toy robot | bear with banjo | luchador | collapsible cactus | sea creature | eagle bottle

The rescue turns into a *cat*astrophe! When Duke makes the jump, he accidentally crashes and wakes Dragon from a catnap. The commotion alerts Gabby Gabby and her dummies, and soon the toys are scattered...and battered...but they are not giving up!

smetics
National
GABBY GABBY
A Very Special Day
As Duke finds the courage to distract Dragon, lend a hand to these members of the rescue team:
Forky
Woody
Buzz
Bo Peep
Billy, Goat, and Gruff
Giggle McDimples
Ducky and Bunny
Duke Caboom

Woody gives his voice box to Gabby Gabby in exchange for Forky. He and Forky are happy to have helped her finally find a kid! Their adventure taught them a lot about what it means to be a toy. And as they reunite with the rest of the toys, Forky is perhaps the most excited of all to return to life with Bonnie.

TICKETS
TICKETS
TIC
BATTERY
While the friends hug it out, say hello to these startled, and oblivious, humans:
this carnival patron
this carnival worker
Bonnie's mom
police officer
Bonnie's dad
Bonnie
security guard
Millie

Page 4
Andy loves cowboys. Go back to Andy's room before he leaves for Cowboy Camp and find these cowboy things:
cowboy hat
horse
red bandana
lasso
saddle
howling coyote
Page 6
Crossing a busy street can be tricky for a tiny toy! Go back to the street scene to find these unusual vehicles:
Monster Truck
Revving Reptile
Lightningbird
Buggy Buggy
Perching Panther
Purple Fuzzmobile
Page 8
What will happen to Andy's toys after he leaves for college? Return to Andy's room to find these toys that are worried about the future:
Slinky Dog
Bullseye
Jessie
Buzz
Rex
Hamm
Page 10
Rex loves meeting new friends! Go back to the Butterfly Room to find these small dinos that look up to him:

Page 12
Wriggle back to the Caterpillar Room to look for these toddlers having a wild time:
Page 14
Revisit Bonnie's bedroom to find these pictures that she drew:
Page 16
Scoot back to the storage bins to find some things that the daycare children forgot and left behind:
juice box
baseball hat
this sneaker
umbrella
lunch bag
barrette
sock
Page 18
As the toys make their escape, they take care to move silently. Help them look out for these things that they won't want to step on or bump into:
stack of wooden blocks
empty wrapper
bicycle horn
maraca
this branch
tin-can telephone

Page 20
Slip back to the landfill to find these metal objects that will be collected and recycled:
hammer
old lunch box
pot
alarm clock
can
golf club
Page 22
Andy's toys are sure to have lots of great adventures with Bonnie. Look around Bonnie's yard to find these things she might wear when she plays with them:
red cape
tutu
fairy wings
cowgirl hat
construction hat
monster mask
rainbow wig
Page 24
Bonnie's imagination is amazing! Bound back to her bedroom and find some things that inspire her creativity, and some creative things she has made:
homemade spaceship
cape
building block tower
this drawing
coffee cup
snorkel
this mobile
book
Page 26
Class is in session! Bus back to Bonnie's school and find these classroom supplies:
counting book
this backpack
this pencil
floor puzzle
dry-erase board
alphabet blocks
ruled paper
globe

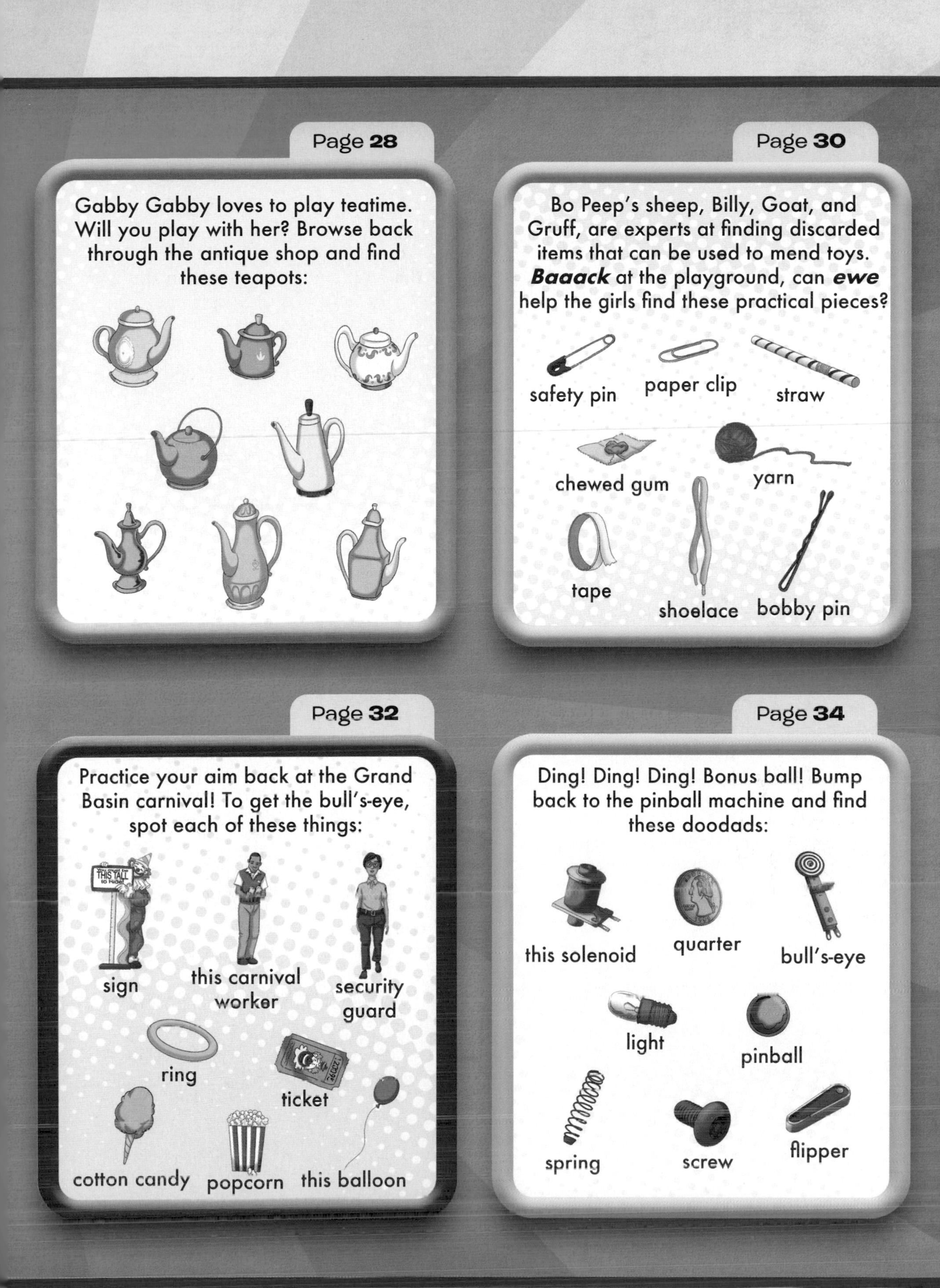

Page 28
Gabby Gabby loves to play teatime. Will you play with her? Browse back through the antique shop and find these teapots:
Page 30
Bo Peep's sheep, Billy, Goat, and Gruff, are experts at finding discarded items that can be used to mend toys. Baaack at the playground, can ewe help the girls find these practical pieces?
safety pin
paper clip
straw
chewed gum
yarn
tape
shoelace
bobby pin
Page 32
Practice your aim back at the Grand Basin carnival! To get the bull's-eye, spot each of these things:
THIS TALL
sign
this carnival worker
security guard
ring
ticket
cotton candy
popcorn
this balloon
Page 34
Ding! Ding! Ding! Bonus ball! Bump back to the pinball machine and find these doodads:
this solenoid
quarter
bull's-eye
light
pinball
spring
screw
flipper

Page 36
Dragon is one feisty feline! Return to the rescue and find these things the cat has clawed or nibbled:
wooden milk crate
stuffed canary in a birdcage
violin
shoe
mouse plush
pillow
chair
this book
Page 38
Step right up to the carnival reunion and find 15 burnt-out bulbs.